TOMI UNGERER
The Three Robbers

Aladdin Books

Macmillan Publishing Company New York

Collier Macmillan Canada Toronto

Maxwell Macmillan International Publishing Group
New York   Oxford   Singapore   Sydney

First Aladdin Books edition 1991

Copyright © 1962 by Tomi Ungerer

All rights reserved. No part of this book may be reproduced or transmitted in any form or by any means, electronic or mechanical, including photocopying, recording, or by any information storage and retrieval system, without permission in writing from the Publisher.

Aladdin Books
Macmillan Publishing Company
866 Third Avenue
New York, NY 10022

Collier Macmillan Canada, Inc.
1200 Eglinton Avenue East
Suite 200
Don Mills, Ontario M3C 3N1

Printed in the United States of America

A hardcover edition of The Three Robbers *is available from Atheneum, Macmillan Publishing Company.*

1 2 3 4 5 6 7 8 9 10

Library of Congress Cataloging-in-Publication Data
Ungerer, Tomi, 1931–
The three robbers / Tomi Ungerer.—1st Aladdin Books ed.
p.   cm.
Summary: Three robbers terrify the countryside until they are subdued by the charm of a little girl named Tiffany.
ISBN 0-689-71511-0
[1. Robbers and outlaws—Fiction.] I. Title.
PZ7.U43Yh   1991
[E]—dc20   91-246   CIP   AC

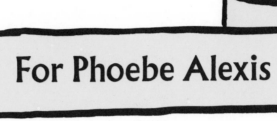

For Phoebe Alexis

Once upon a time there were three fierce robbers.
They went about hidden under large black capes
and tall black hats.

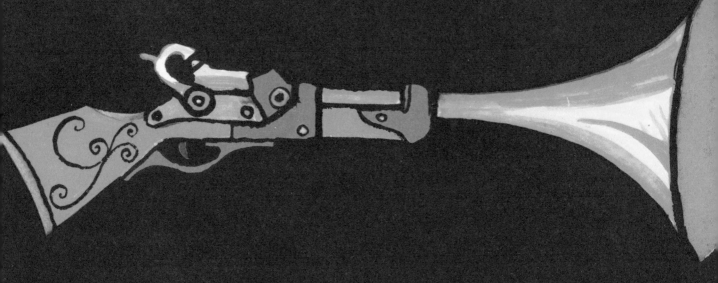

The first had a blunderbuss.

The second had a pepper-blower.

And the third had a huge red axe.

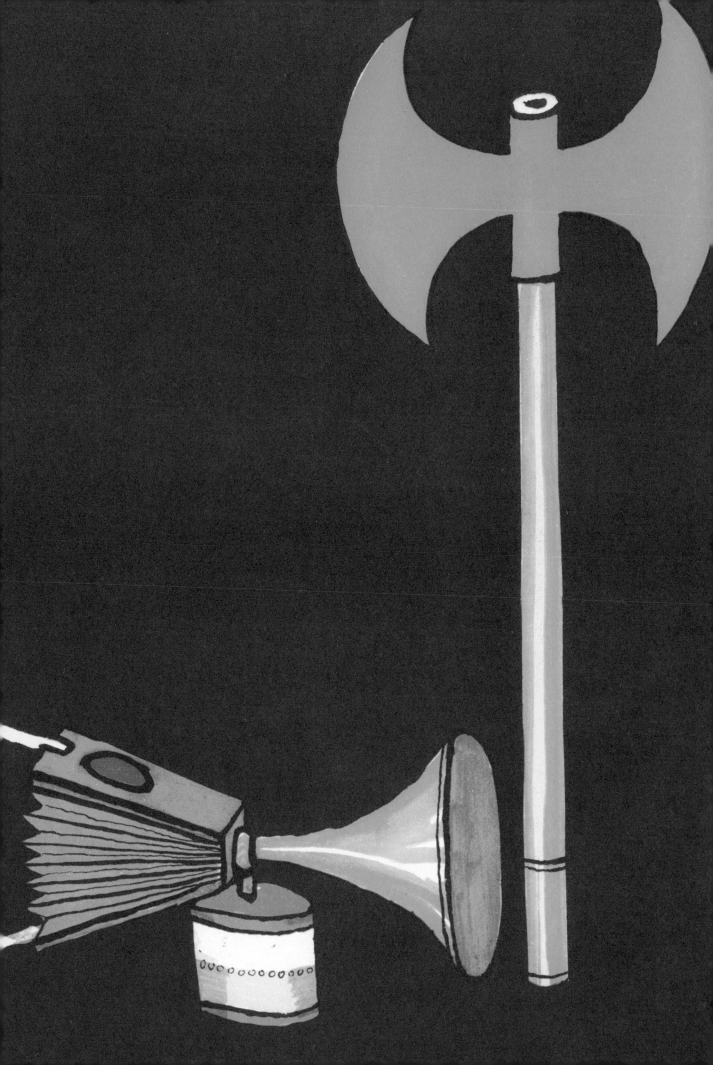

In the dark of night they walked the roads,
searching for victims.

They terrified everyone.   Women fainted.

Brave men ran.   Dogs fled.

To stop carriages, the robbers blew pepper

in the horses' eyes.

With the axe, they smashed the carriage wheels.

And with the blunderbuss,

they threatened the passengers

and plundered them.

The robbers' hide-out was a cave high up in the
mountains.　There they carried their loot.

They had trunks full of gold, jewels, money, watches, wedding rings, and precious stones.

But one bitter, black night the robbers

stopped a carriage that had but one passenger,

an orphan named Tiffany.

She was on her way to live with a wicked aunt.

Tiffany was delighted to meet the robbers.

Since there was no treasure but Tiffany, the thieves

bundled her in a warm cape and carried her away.

They made up a soft bed for her in a corner of the cave.

And there she slept.

The next morning she awoke to find herself surrounded

by trunks of glittering riches.

"What is all this for?" she asked.

The robbers choked and sputtered.

They had never thought of spending their wealth.

So to use their treasure they gathered up all the lost,

unhappy, and abandoned children they could find.

They bought a beautiful castle where all of them could live.

Dressed in red caps and capes,

the children moved into their new house.

Stories of the castle spread throughout the land.

New children came or were brought each day to the

doorsteps of the three robbers.

The children grew until they were old enough to marry.

Then they built houses around the castle.

A village grew up, full of people dressed in red caps and capes.

These people, in memory of their kind foster fathers,

built three tall, high-roofed towers.

One for each of the three robbers.